This Little Tiger book belongs to:

_____

_____

_____

For my good friend Paeony Lewis
~ D. B.

For Heidi, Chloe, and Ben,
for their love, support, and cups of tea
~ D. H.

LITTLE TIGER PRESS
1 The Coda Centre, 189 Munster Road, London SW6 6AW
www.littletiger.co.uk
First published in Great Britain 2003
by Little Tiger Press, London
This edition published 2012
Text copyright © David Bedford 2003
Illustration copyright © Little Tiger Press 2003
David Bedford has asserted his right to be
identified as the author and illustrator of this work under the
Copyright, Designs and Patents Act, 1988
All rights reserved
ISBN 978-1-84895-564-6
Printed in China • LTP/1900/0839/0913
2 4 6 8 10 9 7 5 3

What Are You Doing in My Bed?

David Bedford
Daniel Howarth

LITTLE TIGER PRESS

Kip the Kitten had nowhere to sleep on
a dark and cold winter's night. So he
crept through a door . . .

. . . and curled up warm and
snug in somebody's bed.
Then out of the dark
Kip heard . . .

. . . whispers and hisses,
and soft feet padding
through the night.

Bright green eyes peered
in through the window,
and suddenly . . .

. . . one, two, three, four, five, six cats
came banging through the cat door!
They tumbled and skidded and rolled
across the floor, where they found . . .

. . . Kip!

"What are YOU doing in OUR bed?"
shouted the six angry cats.

"Your bed?" said Kip.
"But this bed's too small
   for you. You'd never all fit!"
      "Never fit?" said the cats.
"Just you watch!"

One, two, three cats curled up
neatly, head to tail . . .
then four, five, six cats
piled on top.

"See? There's no room for you," they said. "You'd never fit." "Never fit?" said Kip. "Just you watch!"

Tottering and teetering,
Kip carefully climbed on top.
"I'll sleep here," he said.
"OK," the cats yawned.
"But don't fidget or snore."
And they fell asleep in a heap.
But suddenly, a big, deep,
growly voice said . . .

"WHAT ARE YOU DOING IN MY BED? SCRAM!"

The cats skitter-skattered
around the room, but they
only found hard, cold
places to sleep.

Harry the Dog was comfy in his bed,
and he soon began to snore.
But then an icy wind whistled in through
the cat door, and Harry awoke
and shivered.

Kip whispered, "Follow me . . . ,"
and he quickly led six cold cats
across the floor . . .

. . . to the cozy bed.

"We'll keep you warm," said Kip.

"You'll never all fit," chattered Harry.
"Never fit?" said Kip. "Just you watch!"

Kip and Harry snored right through the night under their warm blanket of cats.

And they all fit purr-fectly!